Jesup Memorial Library
of Bar Harbor

RULES

1. — **Permanent Residents.** The library books are free to all permanent residents of Bar Harbor.

2. — **Non-residents and summer visitors.** _$20_ deposit, refundable; 3 books may be borrowed at one time.

3. — Books may be kept two weeks and, with the exception of new books, may be renewed twice for the same period.

4. — Ten cents a day is charged for each book kept overtime.

5. — Each borrower is held responsible for all books drawn on his card.

6. — All losses or injury to books shall be paid for.

7. — Mailing service is not available except under inter-library loan.

Apr '00

Three Cheers for Catherine the Great!

A Melanie Kroupa Book

Throughout the text short Russian phrases follow their English equivalents to give a sense of the difference between Catherine's language and Sara's. The Russian letter C (as in **C** for Sara) is pronounced "ess."

A Melanie Kroupa Book

DK Publishing, Inc.
95 Madison Avenue
New York, New York 10016

Visit us on the World Wide Web at http://www.dk.com

Library of Congress Cataloging-in-Publication Data

Best, Cari.
    Three cheers for Catherine the Great! / by Cari Best ; illustrated by Giselle Potter.
— 1st ed.
        p.   cm.
    Summary: Sara's Russian grandmother has requested that there be no presents at her seventy-eighth birthday party, so Sara must think of a gift from her heart.
    ISBN 0-7894-2622-6
    [1. Grandmothers—Fiction.   2. Birthdays—Fiction.   3. Parties—Fiction.
4. Gifts—Fiction.   5. Russian Americans—Fiction.]
I. Potter, Giselle, ill.   II. Title.
PZ7.B46575Th   1999   98-41153
[E]—dc21   CIP
                                                                                        AC

Book design by Chris Hammill Paul. The text of this book is set in 17 point Gararond Medium.
The illustrations for this book were painted in watercolor.
Printed and bound in the United States of America
First Edition, 1999

2   4   6   8   10   9   7   5   3

Three Cheers for Catherine the Great!

by Cari Best

illustrated by Giselle Potter

A DK INK BOOK
DK PUBLISHING, INC.

For Grandma—who started the universe—C.B.

My grandma came to America from Russia a long time
ago on a big boat with a little suitcase, three little children (Aunt Sonia,
Aunt Nina, and Anna, my mama), a little grandpa—and no English.
The man who stamped her passport couldn't say her name, Ekaterina,
so he called her Catherine. Then she had a little English, too. This is the
story of how I gave her more.

It is the early blue of Grandma's birthday morning when Mama leaves for work. "See you at the party, Sara," she whispers with a kiss.

Nellie the downstairs dog is barking at Mr. Minsky's all-night cat. And Monica's dad is drying her hair. Upstairs, Mr. Minsky's toes are tapping on our ceiling. And Mary Caruso is singing opera to her crybaby, Mimmo.

An alphabet moon, left over from the nighttime sky, makes me sing, too. A silly *C*-for-Catherine song. So loud and low I have to muffle my giggles. But there is no need.

Catherine the Great, my Russian grandma, is already awake.

Outside my window I hear her humming something Russian while she shakes out her laundry, picks up a clothespin, and hangs the wash to dry. Then look what I see! Grandma's underpants all in a row. As big as tents and as loud as six firecrackers on the Fourth of July. "Let them shout all over the neighborhood!" she says in Russian.

"Happy birthday to me!
С Днём Рождения!"

Tonight when Mama comes home we'll have a borscht-and-blintzes party for Grandma. A party with no presents.

Last week Grandma announced, "This year for my birthday, *I want no presents!* Подарков Не Надо! I have music in my Russian bones, and laughing in my heart. I have the day and the night, and I have all of you. That's why for me the best presents will be no presents."

At first everyone was surprised.

"No presents?" Mr. Minsky wondered.

"No presents?" Mary Caruso sang.

"No presents?" Mimmo cried.

"No presents?" Monica asked her dad.

"Yes, no presents," answered Mama, nodding her head and smiling.

"How can Grandma have a birthday party with no presents?" I asked. "How can nothing be something?"

Then Mama told me. "A good NO PRESENT can be anything from a kiss or a hug to a game of gin rummy—as long as it comes from deep inside you."

Finally I understood. One thing was certain, though.

Any NO PRESENT for Grandma had to be GREAT—just like she was.

So for an entire week, I watched her. Making vegetable soup for Monica and her dad. (She saved the bone for Nellie!)

Playing ladushky, a Russian clapping song, with Mimmo so he wouldn't cry.

Picking peaches for Mr. Minsky and baking a special sardine pie for his cat.

Grandma even had time to play Gypsy dress-up with me. And listen to all my poems. Like this one:

Oh moony moon
Up in the sky,
You look like a
Piece of pie
If I eat you
One, two, three,
Your shiny shine
Will be in me.

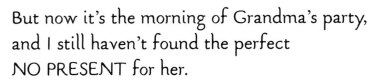

But now it's the morning of Grandma's party, and I still haven't found the perfect NO PRESENT for her.

"Do *you* have one yet?" I ask Monica and her dad.

"We're all set," they answer.

Then I ask Mary Caruso. "Mi, mi, too," she sings.

"I have something really special!" says Mr. Minsky.

And even Mama says, "So have I," when I call her at work.

I look in Grandma's kitchen . . .

And in her room. On her dresser Grandma has a row of saving jars with labels all in Russian. One for prune jelly. One for pennies. One for candy. And one for buttons and little bits of leftover soap.

There are bundles of Russian newspapers and a shelf full of her big, fat Russian books. One book is by someone named Dostoyevsky, Достоевский. She has papers and letters and lists and notes all over her room. Grandma likes to write just like I do. But all her words are in Russian. I look at one of her papers and turn it upside down and sideways to see if I can read it. I know I can't. But I try and try. Then I do the next best thing. I write a poem on the back. If only Grandma could read this, I think.

And right then I realize I have found exactly what I've been looking for—the perfect NO PRESENT for Grandma.

All afternoon Grandma and I chop and shred and boil and simmer the borscht for the party. We fry and stuff and roll the blintzes. Then we smell and sip and pinch and taste.

"We're good partners, aren't we?" I ask Grandma in English, wiggling to the fast and happy sounds of her Gypsy music.

"We sure are, my little Sara," she answers in Russian.
"Конечно мая Саррочка."

Then Mama comes home! And one by one our guests begin arriving. "I hear there's a party here tonight," laughs Mr. Minsky. "For the most beautiful birthday girl in the world."

"Something smells delicious!" sings Mary Caruso.

"Woof!" barks Nellie, looking for Mr. Minsky's cat.

"I can't wait to taste everything," whispers Monica.

And then we do!

"Our compliments to the chefs!" everyone says, and Grandma and I bow together.

"And now it's time for the NO PRESENTS," announces Mr. Minsky, taking charge.

Boy, does Grandma look surprised!

First are Monica and her dad. Their NO PRESENT is a fine and fancy hairdo fit for a queen—or a Russian empress. Look at Grandma!

Mary Caruso and Mimmo are next. "Catherine, I would like to sing your very favorite love song. I have learned all the Russian words myself. And Mimmo has promised not to cry."

Очи чёрные

Now for Mr. Minsky. "May I have this dance, Catherine?" he asks, holding out his arms. Mr. Minsky has brought a waltz. He knows that Grandma loves to dance.

Then it's Mama's turn. "I came home early today just so I could fix up your room. And look what I found behind the dresser! It's our coming-to-America picture," she says, "the one with you and your little suitcase, Sonia, Nina, and me—"

"And," Grandma adds, sending Mama a great big blowy kiss, "our little grandpa."

Suddenly everyone is looking at me. I keep my hands in my pockets and take a deep breath. Here I go.

"Grandma, the passport man gave you a little English when he called you Catherine, but I want you to have a lot. My NO PRESENT is to teach you to read and write English."

No one says a word. Uh-oh, I think.

Then Grandma laughs. "To read and to write English after all these years!
I think now I'm ready." And right then and there she takes out the poem
I wrote this morning in her room. "Please read this to me," she says.

And so I do.

I have a grandma
Sailed here on a boat
Arrived with no money
Or warm winter coat.

Her Russian's a secret
A dark mystery
She speaks the same language
As Do-sto-yev-sky.

If she invites you

лук
хлеб
2 со
добро
дураки
кефир

Don't ever come late

You'll miss having blintzes

With Catherine the Great!

Mr. Minsky is the first to clap.
"Three cheers for Catherine the Great!" he shouts.
"And for Sara the Great, too!" Then everyone claps.

Mama brings out the birthday pie, and we all sing some more.

It is the dark blue of night after Mama has read me a story. Nellie the downstairs dog is snoring. He doesn't hear Mr. Minsky's cat, who has just sneaked out. Mary Caruso is singing quiet opera to Mimmo. And Mr. Minsky's toes are all tapped out.

Grandma has just had a bath with some of the leftover soap from one of her jars. "Today I am as old as all the numbers on the clock added together," she tells me.

"You'll never be too old for me," I say, getting a smile, a kiss, and a place on her lap. I love Grandma's knees and her cheeks and the sound of her Russian.

"You are my Sara forever and always," she says.

Then I notice the moon. "Look, Grandma," I say. "The moon is the letter C. C for Catherine." I write Grandma's name in English: CATHERINE.

"Tonight the moon is a Russian letter, too," Grandma says. "It is С for Sara." Grandma writes my name in Russian: Сарра.

I watch Grandma's pencil go up and down. I promise myself that I will practice writing my Russian name every single day. And maybe Grandma will teach me more.

Then Grandma and I look at each other and smile — knowing that sometimes NO PRESENTS can be the best presents of all.